Mother ~~Goose~~ Bruce

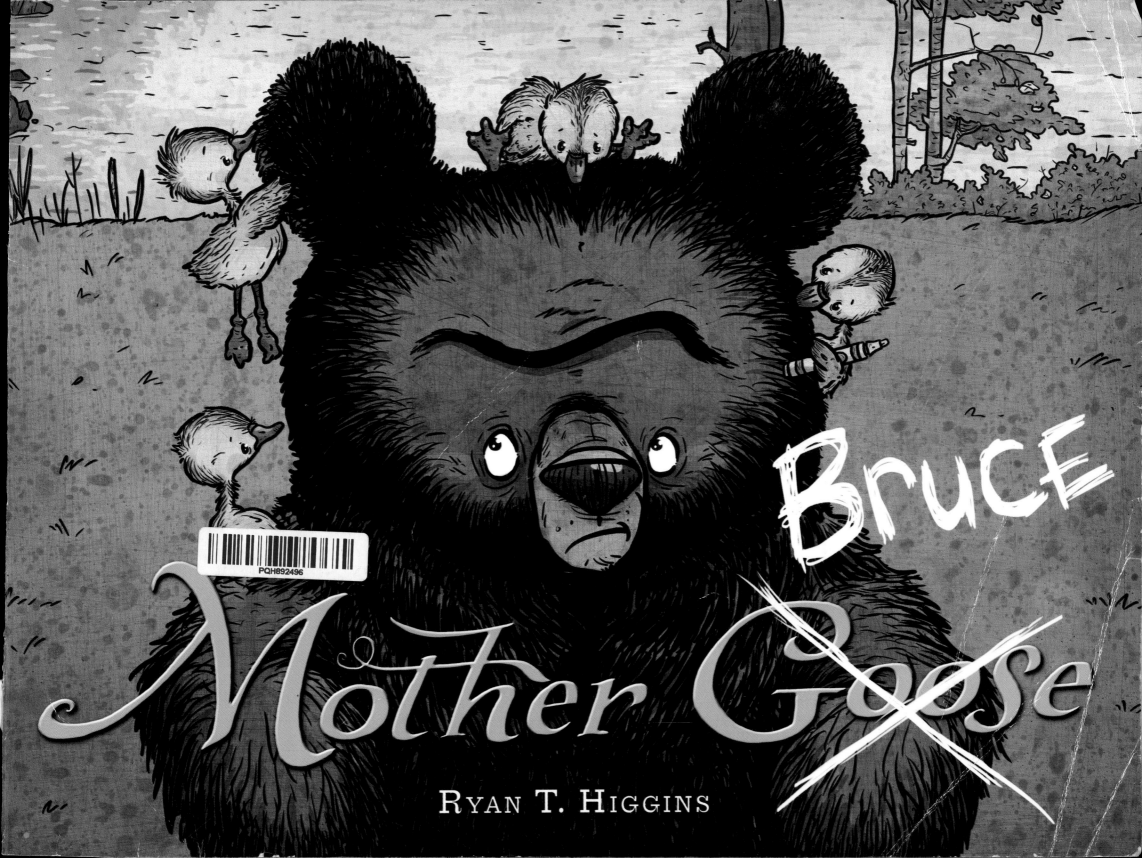

Bruce

Mother Goose

RYAN T. HIGGINS

Mother ~~Goose~~

Bruce

RYAN T. HIGGINS

SCHOLASTIC INC.

For Griffin, the silliest goose I know

Thanks to my editor, Rotem Moscovich,
and designer, Whitney Manger,
for their help in cooking up this book.

ISBN 978-1-338-11430-0

12 11 10 9 8 7 6 5 4 3 2 1   16 17 18 19 20 21

Printed in the U.S.A.   08

This edition first printing, September 2016

Bruce was a bear who lived all by himself.

He was a grump.

He did NOT like rain.

He did NOT
like sunny days.

He did NOT like cute little animals.

But Bruce didn't eat
eggs raw like other bears.

Instead, he cooked them
into fancy recipes that
he found on the internet.

One day, Bruce came across a recipe for hard-boiled goose eggs drizzled with honey-salmon sauce.

So he went out to get the ingredients.

First, he caught
a few salmon.

Then he collected
honey from
a local beehive.

Last, he went to
Mrs. Goose's nest
to pay her a visit.

Are these eggs
free-range organic?

He liked to support
local business,
you see.

At home, Bruce prepared the eggs for hard-boiling.

But the fire in his stove fizzled. So he went out to get more wood.

When Bruce came back, he was met with an unwelcome surprise.

Bruce became the victim
of mistaken identity.

Bruce wanted
hard-boiled eggs,
NOT goslings.

He supposed he could settle
for buttered goslings on toast . . .

but for some reason, he lost his appetite.

Bruce scooped up the little geese
and stomped back to their nest . . .

only to find Mrs. Goose
had flown south early.

Bruce left the goslings there anyway
and went back home.

Bruce was very stern and said things like

And

And also

ROAR!

Bruce could take it no longer and became EXTRA grumpy with them.

It didn't work.

Goslings always
follow their mother,
even if SHE
is a HE and
HE is a bear.

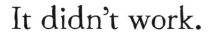

Bruce was stuck with them.

He tried to make the best of it.

It was hard work.

annoying baby geese ←———|

As the seasons passed, Bruce watched the pesky goslings grow older.

Stubborn teenage geese ←|

boring adult geese |——→

Then one fall afternoon,
he saw other goose families flying south.

Finally, he'd be rid of those geese,
and he could take a long winter nap.

Bruce explained migration.

But they didn't listen.

Bruce needed the geese to leave.
So he got creative.

Nothing worked.

The geese would not leave Bruce.